John G. Speed

The Borderer's Leap

and other poems

John G. Speed

The Borderer's Leap
and other poems

ISBN/EAN: 9783337339784

Printed in Europe, USA, Canada, Australia, Japan

Cover: Foto ©Andreas Hilbeck / pixelio.de

More available books at **www.hansebooks.com**

THE

BORDERER'S LEAP,

AND OTHER POEMS.

BY JOHN GEORGE SPEED.

[ENTERED AT STATIONERS' HALL.]

LONDON:
ELLIOT STOCK, 62, PATERNOSTER ROW,
1869.

TO THE

RIGHT HONOURABLE EARL VANE

THIS VOLUME

IS, BY PERMISSION,

RESPECTFULLY DEDICATED.

INTRODUCTORY NOTE.

The following verses are submitted to the public with considerable difference and hesitation. They were written between the years of thirteen and twenty-one ; and as the solace of leisure moments in a somewhat toilsome life, they have perhaps an interest to the author that they may not awaken in others. Still he feels that they are the outcome of a genuine love for whatever is good and beautiful in nature and in art ; and he hopes that they may stir in some heart a kindred sympathy. He offers no apology for the defects that may appear to the experienced and critical eye ; he sends them out to stand or fall by what merit there may be in them, and in the confidence that they will, at least afford the promise of something better.

The volume is dedicated by permission, to Earl Vane, as an acknowledgment of the quiet and kindly interest he has often shown in literary efforts. The thought of associating it with his name was strengthened, if not suggested by the circumstance that His Lordship occupies the hall in which the unhappy alliance between Miss Milbanke and Lord Byron was celebrated, and near which the author spent his early years, drawing inspiration from the scenes reflected in the works of the brilliant and hapless poet.

CONTENTS.

THE BORDERER'S LEAP.*

He dash'd along with lightning speed,
  The Chief of Bord'rers—chief in guilt—
Alone, unarm'd—without a steed—
  His blade was broken from its hilt.
He fled before his enemy,
  His last remaining comrade slain—
The last of all the bord'rers he
  That once had throng'd the rocky plain.
He saw the red declining sun
  O'er his own mountain cliffs that hung ;
It seem'd his feet to beckon on
  To where his every nerve was strung.
And as he plac'd his foot once more
  Upon his native heath—his own—
A kind of pride his bosom bore ;
  His eyes with savage pleasure shone.
The foe, in close pursuit behind,
  Revengeful urg'd the weary steed ;
He gladden'd, hopeful soon to find
  A refuge, spite their skill and speed.
No living form or thing was near,
  Save the wild bird that startled rose ;
Nought the dull silence broke, save where
  She shriek'd in her disturb'd repose.

Then to have heard that distant sound
   Had fail'd a less experienc'd ear ;
But he his head bent to the ground,
   And stay'd th' alarming note to hear.
He heard—like fox at bay pursued,
   With eager lungs he snuff'd the wind,
And, with velocity renew'd,
   Fled the fast-nearing foe behind ;
And rested not till he attain'd
   The base of that long mountain row ;
The end of that broad heath was gain'd ;
   His pace grew gradually slow.
'Twas perhaps his strength but to reserve
   For coming hazards still more great ;
To gather courage and the nerve,
   To yield not to a fearful fate ;
'Twas perhaps his long and rapid race
   His weary limbs had stiffen'd sore,
Or serv'd his stout heart to depress ;
   Or age endurance downward bore :
For by a stream himself he threw,
   That gush'd from out the cliff beneath ;
The foremost foe was full in view—
   Yet gaz'd he fearless on the heath.
As nearer the avenger drew—
   A youth, athletic made—a scene
Most frightful was disclos'd to view ;
   A face of wild and ghastly mien.
Fierce fury, horror, and despair,
   The passions of his bursting soul,
In mingled characters were there,
   Held o'er his heaving breast control.
His dress was torn and stain'd with gore,
   The sign of many a deadly fray,
And his half-naked shoulders o'er,
   In heaps his long hair clotted lay.
His right hand grasp'd his gory blade—
   The sun had crusted up its blood—

His left a kerchief, costly made :
  Red, crimson life-drops on it stood.
He came t' avenge his murder'd bride,
  Beneath the bord'rer's hand who fell ;
He view'd him sink the stream beside,
  And gave a deep, triumphant yell.
'Twas like the weary hunter's cry,
  When the chas'd noble stag, that held
Pursuit at bay, at last to die,
  Sinks pow'rless at his feet, compell'd.
'Twas half like that exulting howl,
  That greedy, savage, joyous bay,
When some fierce wolf-dog in his prowl,
  Secures a victim for his prey.
A scornful smile the bord'rer's eye
  Lit, when it broke upon his ear ;
Th' avenger with that savage cry
  On to the fugitive sprang near.
The bord'rer saw his peril then ;
  He saw he should delay no more ;
Like hunted beast he rose again,
  And quickly ope his dress he tore.
He plung'd his head the stream beneath,
  And on his breast the liquid splash'd ;
Then rose with freshen'd nerve and breath,
  Defiance yell'd, and onward dash'd.
With livid lips and burning brow,
  Full in pursuit the bridegroom rush'd,
Regardless of the stream below,
  Whose waters so inviting gush'd.
His victim disappear'd from view—
  He heard his footsteps as he sped—
The rocky maze he threaded through,
  Down which the fleet-limb'd outlaw fled.
The bord'rer view'd his rocky tow'r—
  Betwixt a chasm deep and wide—
It needed a superior pow'r
  To leap and gain th' opp'site side.

Amid the comrades of his crime
  None could perform that feat but he ;
In rapid flight, full many a time,
  'T had sav'd him from an enemy.
But now his limbs were weak and tir'd,
  Had lost agility and strength ;
Fail'd had the nerve the feat requir'd ;
  He shrunk to leap that awful length.
But, urg'd by nearing feet behind,
  And must'ring courage, from the cliff
He backwards stept—then like the wind
  He bounded o'er the dreadful riff.
He leapt, but not as wont before ;
  His breast met first the granite block;
His limbs and body reaching o'er,
  He clutch'd convulsive on the rock.
Now drops of mortal terror burst
  Upon the trembling bord'rer's brow ;
He quak'd to die ; it was the first,—
  The first time that he'd fear'd till now.
The thought—the fearful thought of death
  Nerv'd him—with one convulsive clasp—
And summ'ning courage and his breath,
  Desp'rate he gain'd a higher grasp.
Just then th' avenger reach'd the side,
  His victim view'd, freed from his power :
" Curse on my nerveless limbs," he cried,
  " The Raven's safe within his tower.
Thou monster—murd'rer—turn thee back,
  Though like a dog thou ought'st to die ;
Turn, unless courage thou dost lack ;
  Fight thine indignant enemy.
Be but yon sun, and Him who made,
  Our only witness, and our friend,
I swear that I'll divide my blade,
  That thou may'st fair thyself defend."
The bord'rer heeded not—he laid
  As all unconscious of the speech—

"Take that to rouse thee then," he said,
 And hurl'd a block across the breach.
It fell upon the bord'rer's breast ;
 Pain'd and insulted by the blow,
"Why dost thou me," he said, "molest ?"
 And rose, "Whence thou—what seekest thou ?"
"What do I seek ? Oh God ! behold !"
 Across the cliff he stretch'd his arms,
"This kerchief once was wont to fold
 O'er Scotland's fairest bosom's charms.
It once was where there was no guile—
 The best of blood is ev'ry spot—
But thou hast stain'd it, ruffian vile,
 With ruthless murder's crimson blot."
"What do I seek ?" he cried again,
 Through teeth that clench'd with rage and grief,
Though life's the cost, yet I'll remain
 And give my vengeance full relief :
To God—and to my bride I've sworn
 This kerchief in thy blood to steep ;
By Him—and her who this has worn,
 My pledge—I'll die—but I will keep."
"Depart ! Stay not !" the bord'rer cried,
 With courage and inclemency ;
Is not my vengeance satisfied ?
 Then tempt me not—depart from me!"
One instant th' avenger paus'd,
 With disappointment stung, and rage ;
The rock he pac'd, like beast that's caus'd
 By hunger in its cage.
But then his brow grew blacker still,
 His lip wore resolution's trace,
"But yet," he spake, "my vengeance will
 Thy name of crime in death erase."
He gazed upon his weapon's hilt,
 And musing to himself, he spake,
"Despair's *my* weight, but *his* is guilt;
 The craven yet at me shall quake."

Then in the ground he fix'd his blade,
  And clasp'd his hands and look'd to Heav'n,
And briefly for success he pray'd—
  That pow'r in peril might be giv'n.
His good steel forth again he drew,
  And backward pac'd to give the leap ;
His hair from off his brow he threw,
  And now he close had near'd the steep.
" But stop thy course," the bord'rer cried,
  " Know death awaits thee when thou'rt o'er;
All further mercy is denied
  When once thou gain'st the Raven's tower."
Th' avenger's one reply—he wav'd
  The bloody kerchief o'er his head,
Then plac'd it in his breast, and brav'd
  The leap once more—defiant sped.
Undaunted, resolute, and bold—
  One rapid bound—he clear'd the space ;
The outlaw's aiming arm seiz'd hold,
  Which else had dash'd him down th' abyss.
There man to man, and foe to foe,
  The bord'rer and the bridegroom stood ;
The arm was held that aim'd the blow :
  A desp'rate struggle then ensued.
They wrestled silent—nor was seen
  That they were sloping slow beneath ;
They met each other's ghastly mien
  And there beheld the damps of death.
" I warn'd thee"—came those words at last—
  " I warned thee," the bord'rer spoke,
The first and final words that pass'd,
  All that the dreadful silence broke.
And as he spoke a fiendish glare
  Of rage and terror cross'd his face,
And for an instant, his despair
  Shone with his passion's fearful trace.
Th' avenger said nought, but he bent
  His head, and from his breast his teeth

The sign of bloody vengeance rent,
   And held his victim's eyes beneath :
And the next moment back he roll'd
   Into the abyss deep below,
Nor loos'd in death his iron hold,
   But dragg'd beneath his struggling foe.
Death-join'd those desp'rate mortals fell,
   Revenge, and crime, and burning hate ;
They perish'd in that yawning cell ;
   Th' indignant stream rush'd o'er their fate.

THE BIRD OF PARADISE.

I wander'd through the grove and glade ;
Through dell and aromatic shade ;
The glowing trees were wrapt in green,
And Phœbus gladden'd o'er the scene.
Heav'n, like a cradled child, was calm,
And softly blew the zephyr balm ;
Odours luxuriant fill'd the air,
Earth seem'd an Eden fresh and fair ;
The birds pour'd notes from every tree ;
All nature rung with melody.
All that's portray'd by fancy's art,
All that could captivate the heart,
All that could charm the eye and ear,
And rouse to ecstasy was there.
Each moment beauties fresh appear'd,
And sounds I'd ne'er before I heard ;
It seem'd as if some magic sway,
Some chain unseen drew me away—
For I could not resolve to turn
My foot back from that beauteous bourne.
Resistless influence lur'd me still,
And further yet I wander'd, till
I plung'd into a forest deep,
Obscure from mortal noise and step.
And, lo ! I view'd a glorious sight :
All glowing with unearthly light,
The forest shone in radiance round ;
It look'd like some enchanted ground
And thousand oderiferous scents
My senses wrapt in ravishments.

Entranc'd upon the sward I laid,
Beneath a tree of spreading shade,
When suddenly, my head above,
There rose a song so soft with love,
So softly sweet! how could it be
The strain for mortal such as me ?
'Twas gentler than the infant's sigh,
That slumbers in sweet lullaby ;
'Twas softer than the murm'ring breeze,
That whispers 'mid the willow trees ;
Or than the falling oars that break
Upon the silent summer lake.
Music of water, air, and earth,
And all the instruments of mirth,
And chantings of the human tongue
Seem'd centred in that matchless song.
Wisdom, and science, and poetry
Flow'd with that wond'rous melody.
All knowledge that could e'er be known
Belong'd to that celestial tone ;
Language, for it was far too weak,
It was not speech, and yet did speak—
It spoke of glories far beyond
The limits of this earthly bound ;
Of joys by earth can ne'er be giv'n,
And bliss that only dwells in heav'n ;
And glorious thoughts through me did flow,
Like angels breathing on my brow.
Oh ! what a soul-refreshing draught
Of profuse melody I quaff'd !
It sooth'd my aching heart to joy ;
With raptures sweet my breast was cloy ;
The floods of bliss through me that roll'd,
Within me hardly could I hold :
Redundant, pouring, swift they rush'd,
Like Eden's fountains o'er me gush'd.
My soul a thousand Lethes felt,
That made each care, each sorrow melt :
c

Their mem'ry far was swept away
And steep'd in sweet oblivion lay.
It was a strain unknown on earth,
No mortal·tongue could give it birth.
Methought I heard th' eternal song
Of heav'n resound her vaults along,
And the sweet harp, in chorus high,
In noble numbers shook the sky;
The loud lyre swell'd the rising tide
Of song, whose waves diffused wide,
And dash'd against the gates of Heav'n;
Methought her quaking vault had riv'n.
Woke by th' imagin'd sound, mine eyes
I turn'd around in glad surprise:
'Twas gone! the sound, the dream was fled,
The mystic light had vanished;
The odours from the wood had gone,
And Spring's green leaves the trees had flown!
What was it then that o'er my head
Had sung while time unheeded sped?
While all the past, midst present lot,
And care and life e'en were forgot!
What seraph had her numbers woke,
Such divine anthems to have spoke?
To man such notes had ne'er been giv'n,
That chaunter sure had been of Heav'n.
Yes! one whose borrow'd wing and guise
Conceal'd an angel of the skies,
It was the Bird of Paradise!

ADDRESS TO THE OCEAN.

I stand upon the threshold of the ocean :
  Of nature's mightiest work—the ever-rolling main !
Deep, boundless, dark ; now calm, now in commotion !
  Furious or still, whose waves roll not in vain :
E'en now, with gentle, yet majestic motion,
  Touching the earth with thy light sporting train,
Thou heav'st upon th' o'ershadowing rocks thy spray,
E'en in thy calmness grand—sublime even in thy play

And I have view'd thee in thy wilder mood,
  Shake. spurr'd by winds, thy tempest-anger'd mane,
Like battle charger on the fields of blood
  Rousing the death-shriek, howling o'er thy slain !
While myriads, whelm'd beneath thy pit'less flood,
  Rent with their last loud cries the midnight heav'ns
      in vain ;
Darting on vessels, throng'd with writhing forms,
And shatt'ring them, like toys, 'neath thy relentless
    storms !

Fierce massacre of death !—Upon that night
  The anxious thousands hemm'd thy wave-lash'd shore
And saw beneath thy fury, with affright,
  Their slaughter'd kindred sink to rise no more !
And while each face, as thine own foam, grew white,
  Crash follow'd crash ! shriek, shriek ! amid the
      tempest's roar,
Till e'en thy rocks, sea-shrouded, seem'd anon
To merge within thy depths, nor view such havoc done.

Next night I mark'd thy changeful tide once more,
  Yet nought to show the ravage there had been,
Save where the dark wrecks strewed thy yellow shore;
  As the moon's rays reliev'd the shadowy scene,
Deaths vacant thrones, thy rocks uprose before,
  And on thy lovely breast creation's lights were sheen,
Which seem'd as calmly glitt'ring there to me
As stars proud chieftain wears for some late victory !

How chang'd ! and oh ! methought a glorious tomb
  Was theirs ; now pillow'd 'neath thy dark blue wave,
Though o'er their rest no earthly flow'rs could bloom,
  Nor mourning eyes rain tears above their grave ;
The flow'rs of Heav'n their resting place illume !
  The rocks their tribute stone !—could man a nobler
      have ?
I gaz'd upon the solemn, beauteous sight,
And deem'd the starry deep a sepulchre most bright !

And now I stand beside thy waves again,
  And watch them gently rise and fall, and sweep ;
There is delight from thy all lonely plain
  To view thee, peerless, liquid-lightning deep !
Sure Heav'n had ceas'd a while th' immortal strain ;
  For could their admiration aught but silence keep,
When first th' Almighty breath'd upon thy birth,
And bade thee free to rove through all the boundless
      earth,

What art thou, restless, nature-spirit, with thy wing,
  Keeping the path to thousand shores unknown ;
Man thrusting by as but a feeble thing,
  Who seeks in vain to call those shores his own ;
Unvent'ring 'neath thy wat'ry sabre's fling,
  Lest thou should'st rise in ire, and hew the boaster
      down,
Or spare awhile, then with a thunder-shock,
Hurl him and fickle fleets on some impending rock ?

Thou king of terrors ! where in Artic pole,
   Wrapt in thine icy armour, thou dost bear
The crashing iceberg—rock, or squall, or shoal,
   Quicksand or whirlpool—dangers dwell where'er
Thy billows sweep ! e'en when the seaman's soul
   Thy smiles delight, and seems thy glassy breast most
      fair,
E'en then thou wait'st, like traitor for his mark,
And with the hidden rock strik'st some unwary bark.

Man's works thine unrestrain'd dominion own :
   His ships but speck thy surface for a while ;
E'en cities 'neath thy waves are overthrown,
   And ev'ry shore grows black with fragments of thy
      spoil ;
Music or horror dwells within thy tone ;
   Thou rid'st in stormy frown or in tempestless smile :
Alike, when fierce, with thy relentless feet,
Trampling the humblest fish-bark or the proudest fleet.

Earth's fairest works, unlike to thee, decay,
   Thrown down by war, or in convulsive throes ;
Man fails, and nature changes her array,
   And these must have their seasons of repose ;
But thou, proud deep ! art no destructions prey ;
   Nor rest, nor sleep, thy glorious bosom knows ;
Thou roll'st, disdaining their unvigrous ways,
Through day, through night, for e'er voic'd with th'
      Almighty's praise !

Changeless in form as the Eternal King,
   Moving yet unexhausted, wand'ring, ever nigh ;
To me such an incomprehensive thing,
   But like a dewdrop to th' Almighty's eye !
Where'er I gaze thy flashing billows fling ;
   Endless, sublime, afar, around, below, on high ;
Dark, boundless, dread, invincible, and free,
Strength, beauty, rage, or sport,—these dwell alike in
      thee

Flow on with all thy changeless pride endued !
  For since creation thou hast held thy weal :
Till by th' Immortal thou shalt be subdued,
  And to the eyes of Heav'n thy spoil reveal ;
Vast sepulchre ! that clos'd since laid hath stood,
  Stand ! till th' Eternal Resurrectionist unseal ;
Till thou shalt echo 'neath th' Archangel's tread
And, whiten'd with the bones of ages, yield thy forming
      dead !

Till cities shall arise as from a shroud,
  From thy dark depths of waters, at the sound
Of the last trump, upswelling high and loud ;
  And earth's clay tenants, rous'd from sea and ground
Marshall'd beneath the great White Throne shall crowd
  Like hosts from sleep, to reach the world's remotest
      bound ;
When earth shall flame 'neath His, the Firer's, feet,
And thou, its cov'rer, cease, as raindrop parch'd by
      heat !

THE LAPLANDER,S FAREWELL TO HIS DYING REINDEER.

My favourite then must thou my heart,
  Must thou thy master leave,
And I be left behind, alone
  For thee to mourn and grieve ?
Fleet was thy step, and bright thine eye,
  As thou did'st feel the rein,
Oh ! thou wast beautiful indeed,
  The beauty of the plain.
But glossy is thy hide no more,
  Thy step no more is light,
Thy haughty neck no longer tow'rs,
  Thine eye of fire's less bright.
For thou art passing swift away,
  My lov'd reindeer so sweet,
Thy wasted limbs and panting side,
  The tale too plain repeat.
I see the death-foam gather fast,
  I see thy racking pain,
And know that soon shalt thou depart,
  And I'll ne'er see thee again.
The hardy Arab loud may boast
  Of his surpassing steed ;
His beauty, and his graceful form,
  His spirit and his speed ;
And he may love to hear his neigh,
  And the quick sound of his feet,
And oft to give him corn and drink,
  His steps may haste to meet.

He loves sincere his fav'rite beast,
  The best of all beside,
And calls him all the world to him,
  His pleasure and his pride.
Yes he perchance unlov'd by all,
  Has yet one faithful friend,
He loves with deep and ardent love ;
  In one their friendships blend.
And oft when white man would pursue
  To rob him of his steed,
He mocks inferior courser's pride, `
  And flees in matchless speed.
In freedom prancing o'er the wilds,
  He laughs all harm to scorn,
Fearless and confident he rides,
  On his trusty charger borne.
The Indian too may high extol
  His wild horse bounding free,—
As streams that from the mountain flow,
  And rush into the sea.—
That loves to plunge through forest deep,
  Through wood and thicket shade,
And hunts the savage tiger, and
  The lion undismay'd ;
He rears his neck, and stamps his foot,
  And proud defiance neighs,
Nor heeds the wild beasts thund'ring voice,
  Nor terrors of the chase :
He fears not 'mid the dangers stern
  Where peril haunts to roam,
He races in uncurbed speed,
  No limit for his home.
The Indian loves his fearless horse,
  The Arab loves his steed,
Exulting in its beauteous frame,
  Its dignity and speed.
They love to gaze upon that form,
  That neck that spurns the rein,

And seated on that trustful back,
  To scour the pathless plain.
They love sincerely—well they may—
  As lover does his bride;
'Tis nature prompts their souls to love ;
  'Tis nature prompts that pride.
That savage bosom, ruthless o'er
  The cold and bloody deed,
That to the helpless captive's cry
  Inclement will not heed,
Melts into tenderness to see
  That object of his joy,
Nor e'er would slay that faithful steed ;
  That loved form destroy.
Though merciless to all beside
  He spares that valued life ;
Ne'er would he bleed the precious beast,
  Or raise the deadly knife.
Each loves his fav'rite but not more,
  Not more than I love thee,
My Deer ! with noble antlers proud,
  And bright and lightning eye.
And if their steed was laid in death,
  Would not they then deplore ?
Ah yes ! they'd mourn and weep for him,
  They'd sorrow, but not more
Than now I weep for thee, my Deer !
  My joy ! my bliss ! my pride !
'Tis pain indeed to see thee die,
  And watch thy heaving side.
Thy precious life is ebbing fast ;
  Thou'rt in the grasp of death ;
Soon thy existence will be o'er,
  Soon be resign'd thy breath.
No more I'll ride with thee the plain,
  No more so swift and free,
O'er fields of ice, and hills of snow,
  Thou'lt bear my car and me.

D

No more I'll stand to give thee corn,
  Or watch thy joyous bound,
Thy step, like music to my ear,
  No more that welcome sound.
I'll gaze upon my empty car,
  And oft to muse will stop
Beside the snow-crown'd hills where thou
  The herbage scant would'st crop.
Thy beauteous form and glossy hide,
  In fancy oft I'll see,
And think I'm stroking thy proud neck,
  Or gazing on thy glee.
And 'mid my vision'd bliss I'll start,
  But not to view thee near,
Then shall I groan aloud to know,
  That thou'rt no longer here.
By thy accustom'd haunts I'll stray,
  When thou, my Deer! art dead,
And think that now my fav'rite's gone,
  Thy form of beauty's fled.
For thou wert fair; how dark thine eye!
  How proud thou took'st the rein!
Oh! thou wert beautiful indeed!
  The beauty of the plain.
But hark! what was that sound I heard,
  So mournful yet so slow,
Like winds that sigh amid the wood,
  The sadd'ning tone of woe?
Ah 'twas thy gasp of death my Deer!
  Thy last farewell to me,
And now, with heartfelt pain, I say
  Farewell again to thee.
Soon, soon, my heart, alas! thou art,
  My fav'rite doom'd to leave,
And now I'm left behind, alone,
  For thee to mourn and grieve.
Oh! thou wast faithful, true, sincere,
  My only friend on earth,

The one companion of my heart,
  In sadness or in mirth.
I lov'd thee truly, Oh ! my Deer !
  I lov'd thee to this day,
For thou wast all I had to love,
  But now thou'rt pass'd away.
Adieu ! my Reindeer ! then adieu,
  But ere I quit the spot,
I'll lay thee down beneath the sod,
  Where thou in peace may'st rot ;
Nor where the hungry bear doth stalk,
  Nor wolves inclement play ;
They shall not have thy loved bones,
  Thou shalt not be their prey.
My task is done ; thou'rt resting now,
  Unmoving in the clay ;
My hand's perform'd the last for thee,
  The last that it can pay.
And o'er thy grave, my sigh, my groan,
  Thy all and only knell,
My heart near burst with grief, I moan
  A sad and last farewell.

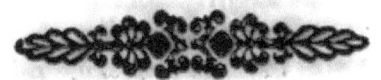

THE MOONLIGHT HOUR.

How sweet by silent moonlight hour,
  To mark the distant mountain ;
Or hear 'mid roses of the bower,
  The play of rippling fountain !
Cynthia with her golden wand,
  The gentle scene steals over ;
Enchanting with her lily hand,
  She sheds smiles like a lover !
How sweet to mark her lightly play
  Upon the glassy water,
That bounds to meet her matron ray,
  Like some returning daughter,
When sports the balmy zephyr breeze,
  Like noiseless spirit fleeting,
Amid the waving whisp'ring trees,
  Her presence fondly greeting.
And by the margin of the stream
  The fairies gay are rev'lling,
As poets say in nightly theme,
  Their tresses loose dishev'lling !
The meads and meadows in their mirth,
  Are waken'd at their presence ;
Where'er they move the dewy earth
  Sheds forth luxurious essence !
The mermaids on the ocean climb,
  From their blue caves upspringing';
They to the wild waves' thund'ring chime,
  Their unknown songs are singing ;
Hark ! from the shepherds murm'ring lute,
  How soft th' harmonious measure !

It startles downcast silence mute,
   And whispers sweetest pleasure !
To catch th' æolian, melting sound,
   Glad sensate Echo listens,
And when she hears it steal around,
   Her eye with rapture glistens,
The crystal melody she greets,
   (Her soul with sound communes),
And from her glowing lips repeats
   Response to music's tunes.
As when the bride's call bids rejoice,
   The toil-tir'd husband hearing,
Answers the sweet peal of her voice,
   Her waiting bosom nearing.
All these together mingling sweet,
   In moonlight softness blending,
The praises of that hour repeat,
   To all their pleasures tending.
In moonlight scenes and sounds what charms !
   How gentle ! how entrancing !
They fill the breast with thousand balms,
   The joys of life enhancing.
The measure of the fountain's gush,
   Amid the roses singing ;
The meadow river's murm'ring rush,
   And sports 'neath Cynthia springing ;
The dewy air, the balmy breeze,
   The shepherd's music sounding,
The rustling of the whisp'ring trees,
   And Echo air surrounding ;
And gentle moon above the whole,
   That looks with eye approving,
On earth so sweetly, like the soul
   Of watchful seraph loving ;
The softness of the moonlight hour,
   The still, yet whisp'ring wildness,
Steal o'er the heart with magic pow'r
   And melt the soul to mildness.

THE DESTRUCTION OF NINEVEH.

Thou'rt fallen! thou'rt perish'd! oh! thou city of
    glory!
Thy people are slain, and thy land is laid void :
Where now hath departed the fame of thy story?
    Where now is thy sceptre of power and of pride?

Thou bird of presumption! like th' eagle thy nation,
    That would build on the rock that is highest her nest,
But the dart of the spoiler reached her habitation,
    And pierc'd and brought lowly her proud-swelling
    breast !

Thy walls and thy ramparts lie levell'd in silence,
    Sad-speaking mementoes of might and of power ;
Thy gates are o'erthrown by the stern hand of violence,
    That ravag'd thy land in destruction's dark hour.

The grass and the wild weeds are spread o'er the dwelling
    Of monarchs and princes,—the high and the great ;
With music no longer the turrets are swelling,
    Nor the walls the wild echoes of wassails repeat.

No more there the notes of the timbrel are flowing,
    Nor the bard is awaking the tones of his lyre ;
And the breast of the minstrel no longer is glowing
    With the soul-melting anthems of fervour and fire.

The minstrel is dead who his lay oft hath spoken,
    In the hall of the noble or palace of kings ;
And the harp of the bard lies neglected and broken,
    While the wild wind plays mournfully over the strings

Lo ! Solitude pensive, in deep meditation,
  Is musing in silence o'er ruins and gloom ;
And wildly and heedless laughs stern Desolation,
  O'er the time-stricken relics of glory's dark doom.

Behold ! in the temple the idols are shatter'd ;
  Like reeds they are broke 'neath the frown of the Lord;
Her kings and her princes lie fallen and scatter'd ;
  Her sons have all perish'd by famine and sword.

The cars of the foe o'er their corpses are speeding,
  And the dead 'neath his foot the charger hath trod ;
Their numbers, all countless, the courses impeding,
  Lie ghastly and still by the blood-sprinkled sod.

O'er their bones and their ashes the foe are insulting,
  And they laugh as they plunder their silver and gold,
While fierce for his prey the wild beast is exulting,
  As he scents up the carcase corrupted and mould.

And the rich bloom of beauty by dark death is blasted,
  And the proud tongue of chivalry ceases to boast ;
The strength in the arm of the hero is wasted,
  And the brave breast is still, and the bright eye is
    clos'd.

For the Lord hath look'd down in His ire and His anger
  On thy vileness, thy sin, and the pride of thine heart;
But thou fear'st not His word, and thou heed'st not
    thy danger,
  And consum'd in the flames of his vengeance thou art.

Farewell then to thee, Oh, thou city of glory !
  For thy people are slain, and thy land is laid void ;
To the land that astounded the earth with her story ;
  Farewell to her greatness, her splendour, and pride !

TRUE PRAYERS.

True prayers are coins cast by the fervent soul,
In the bright furnace of a true desire ;
And at the bar of Majesty divine,
Tried by th' All-Searching in His wisdom's test :
Their high perfection and their precious worth,
By saints applauded, by immortals praised !
Through angels' hands they pass th' admiring Heav'n,
Stamp'd with the image of sincerity,
By seraphs enter'd in the Heav'nly page,
With pen that's dipp'd in life-blood of the Lamb,
Till finally they are deposited
In the great cabinet of the mighty God.
They are th' instalments of the waiting soul,
To build its mansion in the courts above ;
Each prayer that rises from the heart sincere,
One stone more fixes in our future homes.
The first petition that repentance sends
Is the foundation of those radiant halls
To virtue given, when, at the call of death,
She claps her wings and yonder soars above.
The saints in rapture celebrate the scene ;
" 'Tis laid, 'tis laid !" the thund'ring echoes ring :
All Paradise her banners bright flings out
From golden tow'rs, while every string awakes ;
Loud quake her pillars with angelic joy,
Till trembling hell starts frighted at the sound.
Prayers rise and rise till the whole mansion stands
In dazzling glory, form'd by matchless power.
The good man's prayer on his death-bed's the last,
The final stone that finishes the work.

Again what joy ! th' Eternals shout " 'tis done !"
And Jesus says " Father be praised, 'tis done !"
The saints, o'erjoyed, their blooming wings unfurl,
On holy message to descend to earth,
To waft yon soul up to its due reward,
Far from the world of sorrow and of care.
His price is paid ; his passport is the cross,
His prayers have reached Divinity approved.
The soul new ushered to celestial courts,
Borne in the arms of joyful angels thence,
The gates of glory open to receive
Th' immortal guest, and 'mid the applause of Heaven ;
He gains at last the New Jerus'lem's shore,
The land to him of sweet unending rest.
Ten thousand welcomes swell th' empyrean air !
Ten thousand themes salute his ravished ears !
Bursts forth the peal of all the heavenly bells ;
The harp and timbrel sound the theme sublime:—
" Victory and Virtue hail to thy repose,
" For in the battle, conqueror, thou hast won !"
The saints surround ; and, in procession grand,
Bear him in triumph to the halls of bliss !
There with his King to bask in rays divine,
And lose in rapture thoughts of all but joy.
Th' enthron'd Almighty speaks : " Hail, victor hail !
" Christian, well done ! now take thy meet reward :
" Behold thy God, thy palace, and thy crown !
" These are the honours that thy prayers have won !"

CONSCIENCE.

Conscience is the monitor—the guide—
Th' unceasing warner of our erring souls ;
And sin had never won its title "sin,"
Had it not been for Conscience.
She warns us from temptation and from vice,
Like th' Angel intercepting Baalam's ass ;
Nor can we in the folds of heedlessness,
Or inconviction muffle that alarming bell,
That peals right through the very soul with clang
Of loud and startling eloquence.
The sensualist 'mid bachannalian mirth
And noisy riots of the festive throng,
Hopes to forget it, and seeks his relief
Mid flattering praise, and acclamations loud,
At the gay board and in the madd'ning bowl;
Ah ! Conscience, his tormentor, still exults
And shakes the pillars of his troubled soul !
The worldly man in all his blooming pride,
That sits on fashion's never vacant throne,
Drinks earthly pleasures to its very dregs,
And courts delight amid forbidden joys ;
But conscience places in his honied cup,
The drug of noxious bitterness, and fills
His every joy with loathsomeness of gall,
While on his wasted moments heaps reproach.
He in his empty pomp, false-founded pride,
In his exterior seems to be desir'd ;
He smiles deceptive, and shows virtue's sign ;
At his heart's door, when all within belies,
While blinded with his borrow'd light, misled,

Th' admiring world views, envies, and applauds.
Ah! he's but like some goodly-seeming tree,
That hangs its green leaves in the fav'ring sun,
But in th' interior all its rotten stem
The insect gnaws indefatigably;
So Conscience, that fierce insect, preys within
That worldling's rotten heart; which, soon, unless
Check'd by repentance' cultivating hand,
Shall, as that tree, sink into utter ruin.
Conscience! far better earth should rise in frowns
To hoot us; better far than thy reproach!
Oh! thou that fill'st the downy couch of ease,
The thoughtless pallet of tranquillity,
With barbed spears and the ungodly throng'st,
With thousand bitter agonies;
When midnight stillness waves her silent wing,
And black-browed Night frowns from her sable tower,
When Sleep and Silence spread united plume,
Soar o'er the world and seal a million eyes;
'Tis then thou mockest by the sleepless bed
Of tortur'd and self-punished iniquity;
Then, vigilant detective! that thou turn'st
Full thy dark lantern on the crim'nal soul,
Revealing its true blackness;
'Tis then that guilt cowers 'neath thy searching glance,
'Neath thy fix'd eye, and shrinks to see appear
In hideous form and threat'ning attitude,
The fearful legions of his countless crimes,
And his wild fancy conjures up his doom,
Inscribed in fiery characters!
Ah! he that's troubled with an evil conscience
Is building to himself a living tomb:
Each day he adds one stone—he's self-imprison'd;
That Conscience is his gaoler, who locks out
His ev'ry joy, and but one visitor
Admits—Reproach! save, oftentimes, Despair.
Dark is his lot, most awful is his doom,
When Hope, so constant, once her post forsakes!

Death comes at length, and with his iron hand,
Beck'ning his soul to its veternal fate,
Conscience points out the messenger, and says
That th' impatient officer awaits ;
His eyes grow ghastly and his lips grow pale,
Life's prison-door unclosed—its tenant loosed,
Is to the keeper, Death, resigned, who bears
His charge in anguish to the bar of God,
There to receive from th' Almighty Judge,
His everlasting sentence.
But mark the good man—mark his earthly course :
How nobly different he !—his peaceful conscience
Rolls like a placid stream within his breast
That passing music makes, stirred with the thoughts of
    Heaven.
Bright is his lot ; his conscience is upright :
That a conductor on his soul's roof stands
Proof 'gainst the light'nings of all worldly scorn ;
What though the storm may sweep impetuous o'er,
In consciousness of safety his soul
Remains unshaken, and with fearless trust
He battles with all issues unsubdued.
And when Death comes he shrinks not from his touch,
But meets him gladly, reconciled and firm,
Happy to sheathe the sword of mortal strife,
To join his Captain and receive his crown.
His conscience then sustains him, and his soul
Is like a harp that Heav'n plays tunes upon,
Each perfect string unbroken and unloosed,
Though with rude hand affliction oft hath swept,
While angels list'ning to the trial strain,
Catch the celestial notes and shout "'Tis fit for Heav'n"
Death cannot loose his faithful grasp but he
Bears off his cross to the Immortal throne,
And lays it proudly at his Master's feet.
The approving King salutes the conqueror home,
Gives him the harp, the vestment, and the crown,
And points his place amidst the rapturous choir.

He strikes his note, and now another wave
Is added to the exhaustless tide of song,
That never ceasing through the nightless day
Pours round the Eternal Throne.

FRIENDSHIP IN ADVERSITY.

See yon lone echo of a former age,
The silent abbey sinking in decay ;
Where time hath revell'd, desolation roll'd,
And silence reigns, and joy and sound is dead.
Yet still the wild flow'r circles it around,
And the green ivy cheers the grim old scene,
Like children on a sorrowing parent's knee,
To gain his smile that pluck his hoary beard ;
Like Eden's flow'r beneath the cypress' foot,
As if her sad and lonesome hours to soothe.
'Tis thus true friendship in affliction's hour,
Like that wild flow'r encircles us around,
And with devoted sympathy upclimbs
The rugged steep of our repining soul—
That soul that in nought else can find relief—
And takes the shadows from its misery.
In youth we build the edifice of joy ;
Our sanguine breast is fill'd with kindling hope ;
Fortune smiles on us, and our hearts forget
Th' unwelcome sorrows of a coming day ;
And idly dream of endless happiness
In this uncertain world—how false the hope !
Time steals fast on—we, careless, never hear
His pinions flutt'ring on the breeze of life,
Till 'neath his sudden unrelenting stroke,

Our proud but frail-form'd castle falls at last.
We hear the crash, and startled then uprise
From tranquil ease, to view but utter ruin,
The wreck that's left our brooding hearts' reproach—
Our sad reflecting mem'ry's daily haunt :
'Tis then when wand'ring mournful o'er the ruins,
In sorrow deep, uncar'd for, unconsol'd,
True Friendship meets us—in her ready ear,
Our grief-pent soul pours out its full complaint ;
She lists, pleads with us, counsels, and points out
Hope ling'ring in the cypress boughs conceal'd ;
Strikes on her heav'n-brought lyre with magic touch
The strain celestial—love—hope—trust in God ;
List'ning with answ'ring hearts we muse—awake,
And feeling half our sorrow overcome,
We bow resigned, and say, " Thy will be done !"
True Friendship ! thou canst ne'er be truly known
Till comes Advers'ty—then we own thy truth.
Heav'nly physician ! this thy mission is—
To staunch affliction's wound—administer
The medicine of grief—the healing balm
Of Scripture truth—for thy prescription Prayer.
Ours be the same when our affliction comes,
And our Physician Friend—that true one, God.

ADDRESS TO THOUGHT.

Bird of the tow'ring plume and fiery eye,
  Of soaring soul and proud intrepid breast !
Eagle of wing rising sublimely high,
  That build'st far loftier than the clouds thy nest !
When Night her sable curtain draws around,
  And gloom and darkness o'er creation low'r ;
When solemn silence reigns, and not a sound,
  Breaks the dead stillness of the midnight hour.

Unresting Genius ! then 'tis thy delight
  To spurn the scenes of this unvaried earth,
And take on scornful wing thine upward flight
  To those that give thy fierier spirit birth.
Thine on the tempest's wing, the light'ning's flash,
  The world exploring freely and sublime
With a wild rapture on thy course to dash,
  And greet the glories of each changing clime.
Thine 'tis to listen to the thunders deep,
  That swell tumultuous 'neath the dome of night ;
Thine o'er the meteor's fiery wave to sweep,
  Soar o'er the moon, and seek the planets' light.
Gaze on the splendours of the rolling deep,
  And watch the mermaid springing from her cell ;
Or hear soft Echo rous'd from silent sleep
  Sigh to the dirge of music's melting swell.
Thou soar'st on, and as thou passest by
  Pluck'st with thy talons a substantial store
Of food thine eager wants to satisfy,
  From each wide field thy proud wing sweep'st o'er.
Down mem'ry's stream thou dartest to pursue
  Some transient pleasure by delusion cast,
Fled like enchantment from thine eager view,
  On through the portals of the dusky past.
Where in rich romance bloom luxuriant bow'rs,
  And fragrant roses strew the smiling way ;
Indulgence there her wealth profusely show'rs,
  And mirth, and hope, and love, and youth have sway
Oft wilt thou rise and rend the veil in twain,
  That hides the visions of a future state,
Where lie strange shadows bound in myst'ry's chain,
  Bright and dark dest'nies yet unloos'd by fate.
Where ? most advent'rous Thought ! where is the place
  To traverse thine unfetter'd wing shall fail ?
Beyond thy reach, what region, realm, or space ?
  What obstacle, Thought ! but that thou canst scale.
Through earth and air thou dost supremely roam,
  Dost dauntless o'er each interception ride,

And perch'st ambitious on th' exalted dome
  Of Fame's high temple in triumphant pride.
Nor these the limits of thy boundless flight—
  Thou wing'st thy course to loftiest realms above ;
Thou seest the saints in all their sinless light,
  And hear'st the anthems of celestial love.
Thought ! thou that own'st no fetter, no control,
  Oh let me bow beneath thy genial rule ;
Teach me to spurn whate'er contracts the soul,
  And mount with pride o'er folly and the fool.

THE DYING BARD'S FAREWELL TO HIS HARP.

Farewell then to thee oh thou harp of my pleasure!
  Farewell oh my lyre to thy song and thy strain!
To the theme of my soul I have oft rais'd thy measure,
  But I ne'er shall awaken that music again.

Oft, oft would thy chord strike the anthem of glory,
  And the hero inspire to the laurel of fame,
Or in tones of regret would sigh over the story
  Of greatness departed, and beauty acclaim.

'Twas thine to ring forth to the echoes of gladness ;
  'Twas thine to awaken the light lay of love ;
My harp, thine to smooth the deep furrow of sadness ;
  Or the bosom with pity and tenderness move.

And fancy's bright bow'rs grew still entrancing,
  As I rais'd up an Eden of bliss in my song ;
The groves of Parnassus my measures enhancing,
  I rov'd with the Muses enraptur'd along.

Through the road of affliction so darkling and dreary,
  My harp ! thou would'st waken ecstatic my breast,
And when with the cares of the world I was weary,
  I turn'd to thy string and was sooth'd into rest.

Yes there was the draught and the balm so refreshing,
  That fountain of music in sorrow's dark hour!
Like the flowers of Eden the cypress caressing
  Were the notes that charm'd woe with a magical
    pow'r.

I leave thee, my harp ! but oh soon I in Heav'n,
  A note higher still than thy pow'r shall raise;
Oh then unto me a new harp shall be giv'n,
  And my theme shall be nobler and louder my praise

Whilst thy strings, oh my harp ! lie unheeded and
    broken,
  And cease to re-echo to fame or to mirth,
In glory and rapture my lay shall be spoken,
  And my chord pour the measure unknown to the
    earth.

THE DREAM OF THE SLAVE.

'Twas midnight, and the slaver's step
  Was hush'd—he slept 'neath curtain'd shade ;
Awhile the slave had ceas'd to weep,
  And on his couch of sand was laid.

A spirit sudden stood beside,
  And spake : " No more opprest thou'lt be !"
He felt his fetters loos'ning wide,
  And soon his shackled limbs were free.

F

And fairy visions, gilded bright,
   Attractive shone before his eyes,
Burst flushing on his slumb'ring sight;
   He gaz'd in dreams of glad surprise.

The music of his gushing rills
   He heard, and saw his valleys green ;
The glories of his native hills ;
   His mountain cot that crown'd the scene.

" Land of my fathers ! sacred spot !"
   The joyous slave enraptur'd cried,
"Welcome my native rural cot !
   My only home ! my bliss ! my pride !

He felt the sweet maternal kiss,
   The mother's welcome to her boy,
Her loving smile, her tear of bliss ;
   The happy slave wept loud for joy.

"Slav'ry no longer mine," he said,
   "The lash and chain I'll feel no more ;
I cease to toil for tyrant's bread ;
   My sorrows and my cares are o'er."

Vain dream !—he woke—he gaz'd around;
   No mother's kiss, no native cot :
He heard no mountain river's sound,
   Alas ! nor freedom was his lot.

Farewell ! ye scenes of home ; there stood
   The savage slaver by his side ;
Drain'd by the lash his last life-blood
   Was ebbing fast—he groan'd and died.

WAR SONG.

Addressed to the Polish Exiles.

Go ! grasp the sabre in your hands ;
  Your country loud calls for ye :
March proudly forth, ye noble bands !
  To greet the grave or glory !

Go ! Shall your land be free no more,
  But bow in fetter'd slav'ry ?
And shall her sons in chains deplore
  Oppression's heedless knav'ry ?

The hour is come ! to battle rush
  With firm devoted ardour !
Start like the mountain river's gush :
  Defend your country ! guard her !

Let freedom's cause inflame each soul ;
  Your courage dauntless burning,
Mount o'er oppression's stern control,
  Th' inglorious fetter spurning !

Arm, arm, ye Poles ! now strike the blow
  The Czar's vain pow'r disdaining ;
Now quench the triumph of the foe,
  Nor leave one spark remaining !

Fear not to bleed amidst the fight;
  But, liberty inspiring,
Strike for your country and your right !
  Those words your bosoms firing.

To battle then ! and if ye fall,
  Die with that exclamation,

Then shall your death the deed recall,
   Of patriots' reputation.

Then earth shall sound your deathless fame,
   And bright your records glowing,
The bard sublime shall sing your name,
   His notes ecstatic flowing.

And Poland shall be free ! no more
   The fetter shall degrade her ;
And, Phœnix-like, from ashes soar;
   The arm of Heav'n will aid her.

Then grasp the sabre in your hands,
   Your country loud calls for ye ;
March proudly forth, ye noble bands,
   To greet the grave or glory.

———

Chateaubriand on returning from his Eastern travels, being asked why the Jewish women were so much handsomer than the men, gave a beautiful answer to the following effect :—

And wherefore is the Jewish maid
   More lovely and more goodly then ?
Why has her beauty deeper shade,
   Why richer bloom than that of men ?

Why ! 'tis her merited reward ;
   Her beauty by her God was giv'n :
For she despis'd not Christ the Lord,
   Nor mock'd, nor curs'd the Son of Heav'n.

When scorg'd, and smitten, and opprest
   By man's foul hand, and by his law,
Then throbb'd with pity woman's breast ;
   Her feeling mingled with her awe.

And in His final agony
  No woman's voice or tongue was heard
To cast the curse of infamy,
  Or hurl the unbelieving word.

No Jewess 'mid the rabble crowd
  Insulting Him on Calv'ry's height ;
The blasphemy of man was loud,
  But woman wept the Saviour's plight.

How was the dignity of men
  Debased when they slew their God !
But woman prov'd far nobler then:
  She mourn'd, not triumph'd o'er his blood.

The Jewess on the Lord believ'd,
  And sooth'd him in affliction's path ;
While men were scorning she receiv'd
  The word in faith, and not in wrath.

The Saviour more than man she lov'd ;
  While his disciples faithless fled,
She in His death her friendship prov'd ;
  The Cross's foot her sorrow fed.

Lo ! weeping, faithful woman, there,
  Mingling her tears with scorner's cry,
Knelt fearless of the rabble near,
  To the last dying moment by.

While men rebuk'd the sacred deed,
  As though 'twere wasted on the Lord,
The maid of Bethany on his head
  The oil of precious ointment pour'd.

'Twas woman's hand alone that brought
  Sweet balms and spices to his grave ;
She only the Redeemer sought,
  With tears in his sepulchral cave.

His feet were lav'd by woman's hand—
   A woman's hand—a woman's tear,
(Oh she was blest amid the land!)
   And wip'd them humbly with her hair.

And woman, fill'd with faith her soul,
   Fear'd not his garment's hem to touch,
And she that moment was made whole,
   And Jesus hail'd her blest as such.

But Peter had less faith than she;
   That boastful follower trembled sore
To walk with Christ upon the sea,
   Unmindful of His saving pow'r.

And justly Jesus favour'd more—
   More than Judea's men—the maid;
To her affection deeper bore;
   Gave greater sympathy and aid.

He rais'd the widow's son of Nain,
   And Mary's brother from the tomb;
Bade Simon's mother live again,
   And sav'd th' adult'ress from her doom.

And when from death to life He'd burst,
   Had ris'n to Heav'n and come again,
'Twas woman's to behold him first,
   Hear the first words of comfort then.

Some beauteous ray's reflection then,
   Some Heav'nly beauty-giving glow,
A glorious boon denied to men,
   Had flash'd across the Jewess' brow.

MORNING.

Behold! comes forth industrious day;
  She comes with busy active tread;
Luxurious Night flees far away,
  And Silence trembling hides his head.

She breaks that tie with pow'rful wand,
  That binds the clouds in solid pall,
And separated, see! they stand
  In countless numbers at her call.

The tranquil sky, no longer dun,
  Blue lies like ocean when at rest,
And like a silver ship, the sun
  Expands her sail upon its breast.

The dews sweet nature now adorn,
  Glitt'ring like diamonds on her robe;
See! she in state salutes the morn,
  And breathes her fragrance o'er the globe.

Once more the joyous flow'rs and trees
  Wave, meekly gladd'ning all the plain:
They beckon to the morning breeze,
  And speak sweet welcomes to her reign.

And on her tour hath sped the lark;
  She seems a tuneful saint on high;
Hark to her notes ye mortals hark!
  Oh! what surpassing melody!

On wings of rapture see she mounts,
  As hung on high by music's chain,
Seeming to drink the blissful founts
  Of Paradise' immortal strain.

She sings: " All hail! thou Queen of day;
    Thou harbinger of all my mirth!
Thou bid'st me take my heav'nward way,
    And pour my notes afar from earth."

All earth re-echoes " Welcome Day !"
    Birds, trees, and flow'rs their anthems raise ;
Then let us cast dull sleep away,
    Rise, and the morn combine to praise.

EVENING.

Now heav'n puts on her purple robe
    To hail in state the ev'ning hour
A silent softness o'er the globe
    Steals sudden at Eve's magic pow'r.

And nature laves her thirsty brow
    In streams of light, refreshing, sweet,
That from the sun's bright fountain flow
    Profuse her eager lips to meet.

How glorious is the golden glow !
    Those lovely cataracts of light
That down the cloudy mountains flow,
    Gilding all things to radiance bright !

The flow'rs and trees beneath his ray,
    Gaze at the God of Light above ;
The globe speaks welcome to his sway,
    Bound in his golden arms of love.

His last embrace ere far behind
    The distant hills he sinks adown,
His falling sceptre is resign'd,
    And fades away his dazzling crown.

How sweet is balmy Eve! I love
  To watch the melting fire of day,
When Sol into the west doth move,
  And gives his ling'ring farewell ray.

Each tree, each bush, each bird, each flow'r
  Speak praises of her welcome reign—
Of that sweet, soft, refreshing hour,
  That cheers each dell, and glade, and plain.

Oh Eve! thou blushing maiden fair!
  Thou herald of thy sister Night!
When thou thy locks wav'st on the air,
  Surpassing beauty is the sight.

It seems when thou thy face dost show,
  As Heav'n had rent her gates and shower'd
Her glory on the scene below,
  Till earth with ecstacy's o'erpower'd.

———o———

NIGHT.

Now Night advances from her cell;
  With noiseless foot the hills she treads,
And nature dark'ning at her spell,
  She bids the clouds repose their heads.

The trees are sighing on the air,
  As if her austere sway to mourn,
And the dejected flow'rs appear
  Illoyal now to her return.

But Silence joyful lifts his head,
  To welcome in the solemn hour,

G

And smiles as he his sway may spread,
 Enthron'd in undisputed pow'r.

While Solitude broods o'er the scene
 Of quiet glade or mountain side ;
She sighs with musing, mournful mien,
 And mocks Association's pride.

Lo ! Night on her luxurious throne,
 Unfolds her dark yet glitt'ring plume :
In idle pride, stately and lone,
 She sits like hermit wrapt in gloom.

Sedate beneath her feet she views
 The globe in sleep's soft rivets bound,
And dusky nature, like recluse,
 That takes a mournful midnight round.

How stately yet how sweet thy sway !
 How peaceful art thou, Queen of Night !
'Tis thine to soothe the cares of day,
 And herald rest and calm delight.

THE SETTING SUN.

Behold ! how lovely is the view ;
 Sol rolling down the hills afar,
To nature waves a last adieu
 With hand that lingers o'er his car.

While mournful nature gazing mute,
 Sadd'ning at his departing pride,
Seems to return the still salute ;
 Like lovers they—nature his bride.

WELCOME TO THE POET LONGFELLOW

ON HIS VISIT TO ENGLAND.

Hail to our shores! immortal poet, hail!
Columbia's pride, and earth's admiring tale:
To thee we bow in heart, and soul, and mind,
Thou genius of the muse, deep, fearless, unconfin'd!
'Twas but of late thy land was call'd to pay
The homage due our Dickens; now we lay
Our tributes at the feet of him who's won
All hearts—America's most gifted son.
Thou glorious bard; meet heir of true renown,
On whom so late white Albion's cliffs did frown;
Did not thy heart exult as thou did'st tread
The shores where Freedom's noblest race have bled?
Yes, and our nation too rejoic'd to see
In peace and concord such a guest as thee.
Spirit endued with old Prometheus' fire!
Oh! could I break the silence of desire;
My Muse should soar on an all reachless wing,
To celebrate thy praise, thou intellectual king!
Best of all kings, enthron'd, nor mov'd again,
Deep in the living hearts of all true men.
Thou may'st be strange in form, but thou art not
Stranger in soul, Oh, thou whose glorious lot
'Tis ne'er throughout all time to be forgot!
To poet's songs the noblest bays are due;
They fire the soul, the nations' strength renew;
With trumpet voice upon the blast of time
They speak to all men's hearts in tones sublime,
Inciting them like magic to awake;
From slavish dust their freeborn souls to shake.
Longfellow, thou art in my breast enshrined,
The peer the prince, the potentate of mind!
Thee to behold far more than pageant's sight;
But ah! to move with thee were rapture's height.

With one like thee I sooner would consort
Than all the princes that e'er grac'd a court.
Oh thou, who now from far New England's coast,
Com'st to the mother realm thine honour'd host ;
Long mayst thou live in form as thou'lt in fame,
Preserving too like the volcanoe's flame
'Mid mountain snows, thy heat in age the same.
Farewell !   When thou com'st to recross the main,
Strike thou in Britain's praise thy magic strain,
And with thy lyric chords a cable form
As strong as that beneath th' Atlantic storm :
A cable whose electric spark shall be
The mutual thrill of peace and amity.

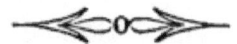

EXPERIENCE.

Stern monitor, austere experience, thou
   With hair that time hath render'd grey ;
Of wrinkled and of stern expressive brow,
   And tear-dimm'd eye of mournful ray.
Thou tellest in the strains of doleful wail,
   Of former glory's faded blight ;
Of pride and pleasures by misfortune pale,
   All withered that once were bright ;
Of hopes destroy'd in ruin's fearful storm ;
   Ambition's tow'ring wing cut down,
When stern Despair show'd his infernal form,
   And Sorrow bent her with'ring frown
Thou draw'st the guiding chart, the road along
   To mis'ry and despair dost show,
But paint'st in diverse hues the right and wrong
   And turn'st man's erring bark from woe.
That frail-built vessel often in the surge
   Thou see'st of dark destruction sink ;
And those unwreck'd, experience thine to urge
   And warn them from the dreadful brink.

ADDRESS TO BYRON.

Bard of the solemn muse and soul of fire!
  I read thy page with awe and deep emotion ;
Did ever mortal strike so sweet a lyre ?
  Did ever poet show more true devotion
To all that's beautiful and grand, and pure°
  In nature, art, or in humanity ;
To all that can the sensitive allure,
  To all that tends to make us good and free?
There is a charm within thy magic name
  That makes even foes of poetry grow feeling ;
There's something in thy well-deserved fame,
  That when we read thy lines our brains are reeling.
Reeling ! what with ?—a phrenzy of pure passion,
  Of awe, surprise, heroic fervour, love ;
Oh intellectual Hercules ! to fashion
  Such spirit-stirring melodies, to move
The souls of men with feelings as of Gods,
  And make them know their place, their worth, their
      minds,
Reproaching with disdain that soul that plods
  Through earth a minion, whom high thought never
      finds.
With thee, pure spirit ! we will roam earth's bourne,
  And foam, and meditate, exclaim, and sigh
O'er Rome's, or Greece's ashes sternly mourn ;
  Bepraise proud fields, grasp time, eternity !
Thou art the poet of my heart : none other
  Can such emotion raise within my breast ;
All selfish thoughts while reading thee we smother,
  And feel with a new principle possest.
Ah ! none can say thine was a common mind,
  Mercurial soul of such unearthly fire ;
In thee grace sweet, and wond'rous force combin'd
  Give magic harmony to thy blest lyre.

We love to follow Harold in his flight
  From Britain's shores, and in his travellings through
Strange lands, and hear bewailings of his plight,
  Bidding to happiness a long adieu.
Or roam with Manfred on the Alps sublime,
  Absorb d in musings dark, impulses high,
Where little but the thund'ring torrent's chime
  Is heard ; whence from those lofty heights the eye,
Surveying human things, far, far beneath,
  Looks down in scorn ; and then how grandly flow
The necromantic words that wrest from death
  Departed forms, to soothe his racking woe.
How sweet the scene when fair Astarte's shade
  Appears among th' assembled fiends, with whom
The mournful one consorts, who stand dismay'd,
  Being touch'd, while she just speaks his name and
    doom !
But oh ! how awful is the sight, when call'd
  Unto their element by hellish crew,
He dies in holy arms, by guilt enthrall'd,
  A noble spirit, though misled, 'tis true.
Next Lara, Gulnare, and Abydos' bride,
  By turns delight us, or inspire with awe ;
While many others have their claims beside
  On our deep interest, but as we withdraw
From viewing these we feel Byronic worth,
  And love the man that can so well describe
The various scenes and passions of the earth ;
  Who heeds not critic's sneer, nor cynic's jibe ;
But proudly speaks as candour prompts his pen,
  Until his teeming page quite overflows
With thoughts both deep and ardent—through such
    men
  The world more noble, more refined grows.
Long, long shall Byron live in classic fame,
  Long, long shall distant lands the time recall
When thou, the wond'rous bard, did'st sadly frame
  Those lofty lays, to hold the world in thrall.

'Twas hard that death should seize thee while so young,
   'Twas hard that so much genius, worth, and pow'r.
Should pass away so suddenly—we clung
   To thee as to a god, when in dark hour,
Thy mighty spirit fled—the world has wept
   A sea of tears for thee, astounding man !
And they whose hearts at thy grand words have leapt,
   Have mourn'd with bitterness thy transient span.
Thou had'st thy faults we will admit, but now
   That thou art dead, we'll drop a manly tear
O'er them, and sadly say, " Most noble thou
   In spite of these !" and still thy name revere.
Then farewell glorious spirit ! may we meet
   On yonder shore of shades beyond this sphere,
And hear thy mane the thrilling words repeat,
   Which have so captivated us whilst here.

EXPERIENCE.

Experience is the buoy that floats
   A warner on the sea of time ;
The place of danger it denotes,
   The grave of folly and of crime.

The sanguine and the hopeful breast
   Beneath that ocean have gone down ;
Their perish'd guilt and glory rest,
   And pride, ambition, and renown.

Experience when they did not heed,
   The rocks and perils of that sea,
Their sad mementoes has decreed
   To mark destruction we must flee.

LINES ON A CONTEMPLATION OF THE HEAVENS

FROM MIDNIGHT UNTIL DAYBREAK.

I have beheld at midnight's deep blue hour,
The planets glitt'ring in the o'er-arching sky,
And deem'd them lovely ; till as morn approach'd,
Slowly they were extinguished one by one,
Leaving my dazzled sight to fast upon
An abyss of comparative vacancy.
Yet while surveying those mysterious orbs,
Drunk and bewilder'd with their lustrous beauty,
I've ponder'd, dream'd, and worshipp'd, till I've felt
They were the eyes of all immortal spirits
That glanc'd on earth for a celestial moment,
And then withdrew to yon supernal vision,
Its limitless Ordainer's special presence,
Who is the soul of everything that is.
Ye stars ! ye spirits ! or ye heavenly mansions !
Ye gods ! or worlds ! things living or inanimate !
Shine on ! shine on ! revealing your Creator,
And heralding the glorious realm beyond ye,
Until your mission cease, as was decreed
At your formation from awaken'd chaos.
And thou, man ! view not yon high canopy,
Repining that e'en Heav'n may be conceal'd
By such a glorious veil,—no ! but exult
That when the black'ning skies shall roll away,
And all the planets fall from off their orbits,
Perishing with universal matter,
Thou, nobler essence, shalt shake off this clay,
That holds thy spirit in its sev'ring thrall,
And triumphing in quenchless immortality,
Arise to Heav'n, eternity, perfection.

TRUTH SHALL CONQUER.

Truth shall conquer ! truth shall conquer !
　Let the liar boast no more ;
All his triumph soon shall fail him,
　Truth shall conquer evermore.

Though the liar be exulting,
　'Tis but momentary pride ;
Truth shall burst in tenfold glory,
　Then Deceit his face shall hide.

They who speak forth lies a fortress
　As of melting snow do make ;
No defence the frail-built fabric,
　Truth shall the vain barrier break.

Then their worthless stronghold falling,
　Pil'd with masses of deceit ;
They shall be to all exposed,
　And the taunts of earth shall meet.

They who win fame by deceiving,
　Are but knaves and traitors base ;
Truth shall show how false their laurel,
　And their records all erase.

Lo ! Deceitfulness enthralled
　In the trap himself hath laid ;
Foil'd for ever let him perish,
　Sham'd and guilty, without aid.

Truth shall conquer ! truth shall conquer :
　Let the liar boast no more ;
All his triumph soon shall fail him,
　Truth shall conquer evermore.

A SMILE FOR ALL.

Oh lovely words ! "A smile for all,"
  Sweet motto of the friendly soul :
Ah ! ye the memory recall
  Of days when pleasure spread control.

We sported o'er the blooming green,
  Exchanging looks of mirth and glee,
Or happy in the ingle's scene,
  We gaz'd and talk'd, uncheck'd and free.

Then in sweet ignorance of the earth,
  Each eye beam'd with a joyful wile ;
Then, thoughtless in our childish mirth,
  We wore by nature each a smile.

The buttercup 'mid dales and mounds,
  With simple breathings seems to call
Our spirits back to nobler bounds,
  Whisp'ring " a smile, a smile for all."

Ye proud who scorn the peasant's door,
  Nor condescend their lot to raise,
Who pass unmov'd th' imploring poor,
  Nor deign to give one cheering gaze.

Behold yon stars of reachless height :
  Are they too proud to look below ?
The high of heav'n, the earth they light ;
  Ye high of earth then cheer her low.

Sweet smiles ! ye precious gems that rise
  Rich from the willing tide of love,
Brighter than diamonds or rubies,
  And precious stones your worth above.

PITY.

Nymph of the weeping eye and loving breast,
  Of drooping form and sad dejected mien ;
Oh thou ! who soothest souls that are opprest,
  And sighest o'er affliction's mournful scene !
Thou see'st fierce Battle nod his angry head,
  And throw destruction's missiles o'er the world,
When Ravage spoils beneath his despot tread
  And Death inclement shouts with flag unfurl'd.
Lo ! Vengeance rides the plain with iron frown,
  And calls for prey, and wields his weapon high ;
But when thou plead'st he casts his sabre down,
  And anger leaves and mercy lights his eye.
Oh ! 'tis not thine of pleasures bright to sing,
  Or fame in all his glittering array ;
Ambition dwells not on thine artless string,
  Nor Vengeance wakes the wildness of his lay.
But thine to touch with melancholy fire
  Thy sweet but plaintive and pathetic string,
The heart with soft affection to inspire,
  Sympathy's tear and feeling's thrill to bring.
Thy presence, seraph, dwells 'mid others' woes,
  Like the heav'ns' bow amidst empyrean gloom,
O'er sorrow's hue a golden glow that throws,
  That gilds the cypress and lights up the tomb.

———o———

THE OCEAN.

Oh ! hark to the sound of the Ocean's wild roar,
As it dashes impetuously over the shore :
Like the crash of the thunder it utters its voice,
And the rocks and the caverns resound with the noise.
Soul-striking the measure ! how grand ! how sublime !
As ceaseless it rolls on with thundering chime,
And sweet and expressive there dwells in its tone,
The praise of its Maker who sits on the Throne.

THE BIRTH OF CHRIST.

Oh ! hail that great auspicious morn
When our redeeming Lord was born !
   Hail, mortals, hail his birth.
He left his throne and state above,
And swiftly flew on wings of love,
   To save a guilty earth!

Ye saints awake your purest fire,
Strike in His praise the thrilling wire :
   Let Jesus be ador'd.
And Bethel's bright forewarning star,
Shines in the eastern clouds afar,
   And speaks the newborn Lord.

Hark ! the wild sounds of combat cease ;
He calms the nations into peace,
   And melts the heathen night.
His banner o'er the states unfurl'd,
He reigns supreme above the world,
   All glorious in His might.

Come, see the King of earth and sky,
In Bethel's lowly manger lie,
   Nor pomp nor state attend.
While joyous mortals rise and bring
Their off'rings to the Heav'nly King,
   And in devotion bend.

Hark to the angels in the sky !
"A light is come to men," they cry,
   "The Sun of Righteousness.
He comes with healing in his wings,
And he shall reign the King of kings,
   And men his name shall bless.

Sinner rejoice ; He comes to save
Thy race from ruin and the grave,
   And bear thy sins away ;

He comes for thee His life to give,
To die that thou may'st with him live
  In the bright realms of day."

Then Heav'n and earth with one accord
Combine to strike the thrilling chord,
  And swell the choral voice ;
Let men and angels in his praise
Their tongues in endless anthems raise,
  And in His birth rejoice.

———o———

THE RANSOM OF JUDAH.

Oh ! hail that great auspicious hour,
  The glory of that day,
When God enthron'd in all His pow'r,
  In mercy's soft array.

Shall burst oppression's iron chain
  That Judah's breast doth bind,
And bid her sons rejoice again,
  And peace and freedom find.

Then shall the wand'rer find a home ;
  That people once opprest
No more in weariness shall roam
  In vain to seek a rest ;

Then all their tears be wip'd away,
  And cancell'd all their shame,
Their curse and their reproach decay
  Before their glorious name,

Then from the corners of the earth,
  Through Zion's gates shall pour
The exil'd race in festive mirth,
  To feel their woes no more.

The harp that long neglected hung
  By Babel's mournful stream,
Snatch'd from the willow shall be strung
  To their Redeemer's theme.

On Zion they their songs shall raise
  With inspiration's fire ;
Exulting in the Saviour's praise
  The timbrel and the lyre.

Then cedars o'er the fruitful field
  Shall wave on Leb'non's plain ;
And Carmel shall her increase yield,
  And Sharon bloom again.

Once more on Judah's hills in state
  Her halls and temples stand,
Her walls no more lie desolate,
  Nor silence rule the land.

Uprais'd in all her former pride,
  Her flag supreme unfurl'd,
Her story shall be wafted wide,
  Through nations of the world.

All earth shall gaze at her renown,
  Astonish'd at the sight,
And tyrants at her feet fall down,
  And monarchs own her might.

And violence shall no more be heard
  Within her peaceful walls,
Nor death, nor famine, nor the sword,
  Spread ravage o'er her halls.

And Judah e'er her God shall see
  Enrob'd in flaming might ;
The cloud of fire shall never flee
  From her enraptur'd sight.

And Baal shall be no more ador'd,
  Nor idols, as of old ;
But Judah, ransom'd by the Lord,
  Shall ne'er forsake His fold.

————:o:————

THE DEATH OF THE FIRST-BORN.

When Night had spread her solemn reign,
And darkness wrapt the silent plain ;
When noise and mirth expell'd their train,
  And hush'd the sounds of revelry ;

Sudden there was a fearful sound,
That shook the midnight air profound,
And made Egyptia's walls resound
  With shrieks of woe and misery.

And fathers' voice was loud and high,
And mothers join'd the dreadful cry,
That peal'd convulsive through the sky,
  And clove the vaulted canopy.

In deepest anguish of despair,
They smote their breasts and rent their hair ;
While spread around from far and near
  Tales of a wild calamity.

For Death with his resistless wand,
Had stretch'd his cold and ruthless hand,
And thousands of th' afflicted land
  Had roll'd into eternity.

Perish'd had every first-born son,
And Egypt's fairest maids were gone :
Her youth and beauty all had flown
  'Neath rigid Death's inclemency.

For from His pillar in the sky
The Lord had heard His people's cry ;
Then flash'd His vengeful sword on high,
  And smote Egyptian tyranny.

MUSIC.

When hearts are stung by care and woe ;
  When pleasure's days are done,
And all that once was bright below,
  On Time's fleet wing hath flown,

Sweet zephyr of the morning song,
  And bright, enliv'ning smile,
Thou lov'st to strike thy chords along,
  And cheerless hours beguile ;

Thou bring'st bright dreams of bliss again
  That shine with gilded ray ;
In mem'ry's stream we lose our pain,
  And sorrows flee away.

And fann'd as by refreshing breeze,
  That steals o'er fragrant flow'rs,
The weary soul may bask at ease,
  Beneath thy sunny bow'rs,

And soar 'mid scenes of past delight
  On fancy's magic wing,
Where fairy forms of pleasure bright
  Amid green foliage sing.

Oh, what beside such pow'r can know
  As music's melting strain,
And speech and ev'ry art below
  May try their skill in vain !

'Tis thine, sweet nymph, to rule the soul
  And breathe with magic spell ;
Who can withstand thy soft control,
  Thy gentle dreams expel ;

E'en demons tremble at thy tone,
  And vengeance fails her fire,
While Saints delight around the Throne,
  To strike the sounding lyre.

ADDRESS TO ———,

MY BOSOM FRIEND, IN LONDON.

———, to me best, truest, noblest friend,
I swear that nought but death itself shall end
Our union, in such hours delightful form'd,
When passion's spring by earliest youth was warm'd.
Ah! ne'er shall I forget the happy time,
Ere yet exceeding boyhood's blissful prime,
The long, long summer's nights, the pleasant talks,
The merry pastimes, and the rural walks,
That I and thee in sweet communion shar'd,
Our hearts on fire, by sorrow unimpair'd.
Yes! well do I recall those distant days,
That stand out clear 'midst life's entangling maze,
When link'd by mutual concord's magic chain,
We dreamt of bliss alone, nor thought of pain;
And mem'ry lingers fondly o'er those themes,
Th' exhaustless subjects of our boyish dreams,
When Cromwell's, Nelson's, Wellington's bright fame,
Stirr'd in our hearts the hank'ring for a name:
And Shakespeare, Milton, Byron, all review'd,
Seem'd as we talk'd with tenfold charms endued.
Alas! those happy days are now no more;
Ah! now in vain their absence we deplore;
Relentless Time no throb of pity knows,
Unheeding in his course man's keenest throes.
A few brief hours we snatch'd of fleeting joy,
Ere he appear'd the mirage to destroy.
But now as fast our boyish days subside,
Let youthful fire give place to manly pride;
Though ne'er as wont we may consort, yet still
There's pleasure up life's variegated hill,
And though not now, in manhood we may meet
With hearts that still shall for each other beat.
Then let us meet with higher, nobler aims,

And seek by good to consecrate our names.
Let us breathe out in the inspiring page
'Gainst wrong and tyranny volcanic rage.
Let us unite 'gainst false conceits and forms
And them assail, spite faction's fiercest storms.
Let us determine that we will not bow
To creeds or customs that no truth allow.
But above all let us our course maintain,
Of stubborn rectitude, of virtue plain,
Nor from that course desist whate'er betides,
Though fate opposes and though man derides.
Adieu! my noble friend, to thee adieu!
To me as am'rous knight thou hast been true,
True as magnetic needle to the pole,
As stars to heav'n when black'ning clouds do roll.
Thy mem'ry deep shall in my heart endure,
Type of the true, the passionate, the pure!
Though strange may, be and chequer'd my career,
Thy image there shall live unsullied, clear.
And if affliction be my hapless lot,
That still shall prove one bright consoling spot
In life's wild desert—that preserve my soul
Still fresh and green, though storms above me roll,
And ere the dust its kindred clay reclaim
My dying lips shall falter out thy name.

INGRATITUDE.

E'en as a barren piece of earth,
   Which, when the seed profuse is thrown,
Declines the produce to give birth,
   But yields forth weeds and thorns alone.

So of ingratitude the heart,
   When seeds of plenteous love are thrown,
Doth in return, but weeds impart
   Of noxious evil's growth alone.

ON THE CROSS

—o—

Oh, weary Christian ! when thou'rt burden'd sore
   With heavy trouble's, huge, soul-burd'ning load ;
When trials stern and strong temptations pour,
   Hold up the Cross—the signal for thy God,

Lo ! Christ is near, and when He views that sign
   Erected firmly on the dome of Faith,
His summon'd spirit soon shall stand by thine
   To guard thee his protecting arms beneath.

The Cross shall be thy trustful bridge secure,
   When thou art call'd to cross dark Jordan o'er ;
Thy life-buoy on that wave, preserver sure,
   And safely thou shalt reach the distant shore.

In the fierce tempest of Jehovah's ire,
   When meteors and thunders of His vengeance fly ;
The Cross, conductor of that lightning fire,
   The storm thy soul shall pass in mercy by.

And lo ! when at the gates of Paradise,
   Hold up the Cross, the sign of victory,
The saints with shouts that pledge shall recognize,
   And hail thee to the New Jerus'lem, free.

And when that testimonial thou shalt bear
   Up to the throne of Jesu's bright renown,
The Lamb of God in love shall greet thee there,
   And for the cross exchange an endless crown.

TO THE MOON.

Majestic moon ! in silv'ry light,
Exulting in thy lurid might,
   Thee rapt'rous I behold.
Thou spread'st thy beauteous creston high,
Gilding with glory all the sky,
   Hung like a gem of gold.

Thy face shines on the silent plain,
Or dances on the glassy main;
   Reflecting there thy form ;
Thou sitt'st above the deep, serene,
And view'st beneath the passing scene,
   The same in calm or storm.

And when creation's voice is mute,
Save where yon shepherd's murm'ring lute
   Wakes solemn echoes round ;
Or where the shady rustling trees,
Waving upon the nightly breeze,
   Whisper with gentle sound.

Celestial Queen ! on silent air
Thou lov'st to wave thy golden hair,
   Thy wings upon the night ;
And walk where midnight stillness reigns,
And shine upon deserted plains,
   And cheer them with thy light.

And when the travl'ler wends his way,
Far from his native home astray,
   Thou bidd'st his heart rejoice ;
To those who solitary roam,
Without a rest without a home,
   Thou hast a welcome voice.

And oh ! fair Moon, I love to gaze
With thoughts poetic on thy face ;
   Thou wrapp'st in dreams my soul :

I love to see the heav'ns along
Amidst the planets' countless throng,
  Thy form majestic roll.

I love to watch thee sailing high,
Then plunging far beneath the sky,
  Lost in a sea of night ;
Then bursting from beneath the clouds,
Undimmed by those livid shrouds,
  Once more disclose thy light.

AFFLICTION.

While standing on the ocean shore,
  A distant wave came rolling on,
Which seem'd stupendous in its pow'r,
  Yet parted at my feet anon.

Thus meet Affliction's threat'ning shoal,
  Nor from its mighty force retreat ;
It shall not overwhelm thy soul,
  But pow'rless break beneath thy feet.

TO THE STARS.

Ye faithful subjects of the midnight hour,
  That glitter am'rous in the darkling sky,
Like golden roses in a livid bow'r,
  Like Eden's growth 'neath cypresses, on high,

As from the sky ye ever seem to spring,
  Like aureate birds that there have hidden nest,
To move and fluttter—and anon to sing
  The sweetest echoes of the anthems blest.

PRARYER.

Oh ! what a noble pow'r is pray'r,
Inestimable, rich, and fair,
  A boon to mortals giv'n ;
It is the golden key whereby
The Christian opes the treasury
  Of endless stores in Heav'n

It is a fort impregnable,
Against the fiery darts of Hell,
  Immutable, secure.
And when the voice of pray'r he hears,
Satan with all his legion fears,
  And feels its vict'ry sure.

And when affliction's billows roll,
And half o'erwhelm the Christian's soul,
  He pours his heart in pray'r.
Be it one heartfelt tear or word,
It ne'er ascends to Heav'n unheard,
  But is recorded there.

It bursts affliction's iron bar,
And soars, sublime in rapture, far
  From this vile earth away.
And like an eagle in its flight,
It pierces through the depths of night,
  And cleaves the realms of day.

And when the pilgrim on his road,
Weary and fainting with his load,
  Near sinks his cross beneath,
It cheers his heart and nerves new strength,
And guides him to his journey's length.
  Across the stream of death.

LINES ON THE EVE OF MY 21st. BIRTHDAY

This night I bid a last adieu
  To boyhood's fast-receding days,
To-morrow must my birth renew,
  And meet my life's maturer phase.

Though young I be yet o'er my soul
  An age in sob'ring thought has past,
And now when reaching manhood's goal
  I 'gin to feel the truth at last.

Too much in thought I have employ'd
  The hours I should have better spent ;
I look back on the aching void,
  And on my youth's death-bed repent.

That thought has been like furrow'd seed
  Sown in the wrinkles of my brow,
A bounteous harvest shall succeed,
  And action be my polestar now.

Then from this time hence all vain joys,
  All friv'lous thoughts, distracting aims ;
These are but baubles fit for boys ;
  A nobler field my manhood claims.

Oh Time ! as I approach the hour,
  My spirit fain would thee beguile ;
From thee a moments pause implore.
  That I might meditate awhile.

And oh ! it is a thought sublime
  My sun shall sink as 'twere to-night,
But in the antipodes of time—
  My manhood—rise with tenfold light.

This night to me doth seem endued
  With something hallow'd, solemn, strange ;

No cav'lling, friv'lous thoughts intrude,
  My sterner feelings to derange.

I feel the dawn of coming pow'r
  And like the eagle I exult,
Though thunderclouds around me low'r,
  I'll glory in their wild tumult.
I hate this calm, this fest'ring peace,
  That stagnates round the weary soul!
In danger's self I'd seek release,
  But spurn this narrow world's control.

Soon shall I start upon the world,
  Prepared to meet its smile or sneer;
Soon, Silence' mantle from me hurl'd,
  A full-arm'd combatant appear.

Then hail my manhood! doubly hail!
  A new existence lies in thee;
Far better aiming high, to fail,
  Than plod thus on ingloriously.

Perchance in some far coming years,
  My chord may stir the hearts of men;
And souls of yet unborn compeers,
  Leap to the lightnings of my pen.

FAITH.

Faith's pow'r divides affliction's sea,
  Like Moses' Heav'n enchanted wand,
And dryshod, from those billows free,
  On New Jerus'lem's shore we land.

CONVICTION.

Conviction smites the sinner's heart,
  Like Moses' wondrous rod,
When lo! in twain that rock doth part,
  And flows repentance unto God.

ENGLAND AND AMERICA.

—o—

Written During the Alabama Dispute.

—o—

And must it be that we must fight
  Who hold the ends of earth in sway ;
We, who, if we but join'd our might,
  Could keep the world combin'd at bay ?

Must we, earth's capitals, whose star
  Of glory lightens all the main,
Meet like two thunderclouds of war,
  Dissolving in a bloody rain ?

Must *we of all the earth among,*
  Whose race, whose lineage are the same ;
We of one heart, one mind, one tongue,
  We, brothers, breathe war's hostile flame ?

Spite all these ties, must there be riv'n,
  'Twixt us and thee that breach abhorr'd,
Which, like the pass to houris' heav'n,
  Can but be bridg'd by naked sword ?

Ah no ! perchance volcanic rage,
  Our kindred shores has severed wide,
But our true hearts from age to age,
  Shall war's volcano ne'er divide.

Bound like the twins of Siam we,
  Our ligature th' electric cable ;
And if that union sever'd be,
  'Twill, if not slay, us both disable.

Twixt us no strife shall intervene
  To mar our glorious brotherhood ;
Th' Atlantic wide may roll between,
  But ne'er that sea—a sea of blood.

HOPE.

Oh Hope ! that fair celestial maid,
In animating smiles arrayed,
  With sweet soul-soft'ning lyre :
She with delusive charms doth shed,
Round the desponded weary head,
  And doth the soul inspire.

She wakes us with her magic wand,
And leads us to the fairy land
  Of future pleasures bright.
And then our cares we bid adieu,
And gaze enchanted at the view,
  In rapture and delight.

She binds the heart with soft control,
And cheerful songs unto the soul
  Of promised pleasure pours;
And at her presence dark Despair
Shrinks back into his fiendish lair,
  And in the distance roars.

Woke by her sweet melodious lyre,
We soar on fancy's wings of fire,
  To joys that seem all true,
And walk 'midst shades of sunny bow'rs,
Through fragrant paths of scatter'd flow'rs
  Of ev'ry scent and hue.

Then Hope through life my path shall cheer,
Shall charm mine heart and please mine ear,
  And Sorrow's hours beguile.
And through Affliction's depths of night,
Shine, thou fair star ! unmarr'd thy light
  E'er on my spirit smile.

APPEAL AGAINST THE DESTRUCTION OF SHAKESPEARE'S HOUSE.

AIR :—" *Woodman spare that Tree.*"

England ! spare that place ;
   Touch not a single stone,
For 'tis the hallow'd trace
   Of highest glory gone.

There Shakespeare woke the strain
   Fix'd for undying lot ;
England, let it remain ;
   Destroy, destroy it not !

Shall that familiar spot
   That *his* great name recalls
Have desecrated lot,
   And sink its honour'd walls ?

Forbear ! forbear that hand
   That would that spot lay low !
Still let it crown our land ;
   Forbear ! forbear the blow !

Our noblest poet there
   Hath liv'd, and mus'd, and sung ;
High thoughts were spoken there ;
   Since breath'd by ev'ry tongue.

There all the fires have blaz'd
   Of merit and of worth ;
There songs of Heav'n were rais'd
   That have astonish'd earth.

Then by that noble name,
   The proudest yet enroll'd
In calendars of fame,
   Those hallow'd walls uphold.

As one true monument
   Of him whom kings adore,
With all his honours blent,
   Stand thou for evermore !

Stand ! though the storm may rage,
   Firm and immovable,
And many a future age
   Of Shakespeare's birth-place tell.

But thou the storm shalt brave,
   Sacred and honour'd spot !
While we've a hand to save,
   They shall destroy thee not.

OBSCURE GENIUS.

There is a flow'r, a sensate flow'r,
   That flashes forth electric light
Unseen upon the darkling hour,
   And solitary 'neath the night.

So genius oft obscure unknown,
   Wakes lofty inspiration's fire ;
Worth oft in quiet and alone,
   Strikes the deep flashes of her lyre.

And many a bard has struck his strain,
   Giv'n fervour, fire, and feeling, birth ;
Greatness has liv'd confin'd, unseen,
   Unheard of through th' unconscious earth.

True merit doom'd unseen to shine,
   Has soar'd to proud yet praiseless height ;
In secret men have liv'd to pine,
   In lustrous yet unnotic'd light.

Men that th' admiring world had known,
   Whose names through time had faded not,
Had fame their blast of honour blown ;
   But ignorance gave unlaurell'd lot.

THE STORMY CLOUD.

See yon black cloud, like some unruly steed,
That proudly rides unhalter'd o'er the plain !
He plants his scornful foot upon the skies,
And tramples heedless on the flying sun.
His livid wing he waves upon the air,
In awful grandeur, in exulting might ;
O'er Heav'ns' wide field, uncurb'd and uncontroll'd,
He rides and roars, and shakes th' emp'yrean vault.
Hark to his snort ! that loud, that deaf'ning roar
That spreads far-echoing o'er the unbounded sphere;
Fierce balls of lightning from his gaping mouth
He belches forth in heat of bursting wrath.
Oh ! gloomy cloud ! in nature where shall we
Behold a scene more grand and more sublime ?
What art thou like ? thou awful prodigy !
The battlement of heav'n, the skies' stronghold;
The thunder is th' artillery of thy walls :
The winged lightning is thy cannon's flash !

MUSIC.

Like the mhoonlight to the ocean,
    Whose waves it seems to lull,
Is Music's healing motion
    To the heart with sorrow full.

Sweet when Beauty sweeps the strings,
    To charm the mourner's ear ;
Grief before the sound takes wings ;
    Forms of magic bliss draw near.

Dreams of youth and long-lost pleasure,
    Relight, the faded eye ;
Music ! at thy heav'nly measure,
    Vanquish'd sorrow can but fly.

ON THE DEATH OF HENRY KIRKE WHITE

WHO DIED IN HIS 21ST YEAR.

Bard of the lofty soul and wing inspir'd,
 Of thought sublime and inspiration's tongue,
Great minstrel thou, by highest genius fir'd ;
 Laid low when on the sweetest note of song ;

And thine own talent was the mace that fell'd
 Thee to the ground and thrust thee to the tomb ;
Thy peal of fame was but the note that swell'd
 The deep death-wail that rose upon thy doom ;

And like the vampire, fatal, foul, and fell ;
 That fans its prey, yet drains his blood the while,
So did thy treach'rous genius flatt'ring tell
 Of future fame, yet slew thee with a smile.

Like the night's songster pour'd thy muse her breath
 E'en while her bosom touch'd the thorn of death,
And as the swan that feels her final pang,
 Her own deep dirge-note promise woke and sang.

TO A BEAUTIFUL YOUNG LADY.

All beauteous as thou art, fair maid !
 I ne'er could fall in love with thee ;
And why ?—if Cupid thee beheld,
 E'en Cupid's self would smitten be.

ADDRESS TO SEAHAM HARBOUR,

MY BIRTHPLACE.

—o—

Hail! Seaham, hail! beloved spot of earth,
Belov'd because the spot that gave me birth;
Long round thy coast shall clust'ring mem'ries twine,
Of happy days I've spent with thee and thine;
What though in form I may not e'er be nigh,
My spirit, bird-like, e'er to thee shall fly;
Far lands perchance may hence my bosom fire,
But ne'er such pure delight as thee inspire;
Thee with such thronging recollections rife,
Where erst I spent the honeymoon of life;
Obscure, remote, neglected though thou be,
Thou still, sweet spot! hast charms untold for me;
The brawling world around may madly roar,
But ne'er can wean me from thy peaceful shore.
Yet not alone with happy dreams thou'rt fraught;
Alas! thou stirr'st a spring of mournful thought;—
On yonder hill where stands the House of Pray'r,
And pious feet at eventide repair,
A mother's ashes rest—a mother such
As Heav'n could ne'er excel, nor man extol too much:
Yon simple vault 'neath which her dust is hid,
Records more worth than hero's pyramid,
And though beneath yon modest stone she lies,
Within my heart of hearts she never dies.—
But turn we sadly from this hallow'd ground
To yonder rise by princely mansion crown'd,
And pause to contemplate th' auspicious fane,
The noble heirloom of the house of Vane,
(Th' exalted scion of whose titled line
Now smiles on me, the vot'ry of the Nine,
With his illustrious name my page endues,
And soars the guardian genius of my muse)
For there it stands a monument of fame,
The record of th' immortal Byron's name.

There in yon room, to strangers' eyes denied,
'I he noble poet clasp'd his new-made bride.;
There did he dwell—and there those deathless lays
Compos'd, that thrill'd with wonder and amaze ;
And down yon slope in yon plantation deep,
Through which the meand'ring stream doth murm'ring
      creep,
There did he sit—there oft his footsteps stray,
And dream, soul-wrapt, th' unconscious hours away.
Ah ! dear to me that calm sequester'd grot,
Preserv'd, untouch'd—a consecrated spot :
Oh may no rude defacing hands pass o'er ;
But may it stand for ages as of yore ;
More classic ground the world could not bestow,
That stream a second Helicon doth flow.
Then pause again where stand two hawthorn trees,
And learn the mournful tale convey'd by these :—
Lo ! as I gaze what means this vision strange ?
These hawthorn trees their forms obscurely change ;
As in the tales of Genii I see
Two mortals bodied forth from either tree,
Two mortals—male and female—there they stand
In anguish deep each clasps the other's hand :
In one long last embrace they ling'ring part,
Then from each other turn—with broken heart.
I gaze spell-bound—but now the dream is o'er ;
The hawthorn trees resume their place once more.
I pause, long pond'ring on their mournful lot,
Heave but one sigh, and tearful quit the spot.
What means this dream ?—Alas !—where stand those
      trees,
(And where deep human sighs pervade the breeze,)
The hapless Byron parted from his wife,
To whom in yon proud hall he join'd his life ;
At least such is the tale—or true or not
(Though some there be who say 'tis not the spot)
Yet still would I the cherish'd dream pursue,
And fain believe the fond tradition true.

Yes! Seaham, yes! though thou may'st lie obscure,
Thy name with *his* through ages shall endure :
Thy cliffs shall stand his monuments of fame,
And every wave shall whisper of his name,
And oft in fancy shall his form be seen
Haunting the spots where he so oft has been ;
And travellers shall pause thy scenes among,
To point and say :—"Here Byron liv'd and sung."
But what avails this humble praise of mine,
Since kings might homage do at such a shrine ;
Enough for me, if, born where he hath been,
Treading where he hath trod—each hallow'd scene ;
If I, perchance his spirit hov'ring near,
Breathing, as he hath breath'd, that atmosphere,
While bending at that shrine with prostrate lyre,
Have caught one spark of his ethereal fire.
But ere to Seaham's shores we bid adieu
Pause we and gaze on yon broad ocean blue,
Touching the earth, or mingling with the sky,
A wat'ry universe, below, on high.
Oft have I rov'd those glorious rocks along,
And listened, awestruck, to its billowy song ;
Or seated on those pinnacles alone,
My spirit's empire view'd as from a throne,
While e'en as o'er its breast the waves did roll,
Have strange deep musings pass'd athwart my soul.
Seaham ! thy name shall in my mem'ry dwell,
And of my birth, her death, fame, beauty tell ;
Till call'd from earth to quit my cumb'ring clay,
And 'neath thy soil perchance my kindred ashes lay ;
Thou gavest me my first—my latest breath
Will I give thee, and tune thy praise till death.

NOTES.

a.—THE BORDERER'S LEAP.—Page 9

This composition is founded upon a prose tale which the author read in a work called the "Casquet," now, he believes, out of print. The Borderer was the chief of a clan of desperate ruffians who bore that name on account of their inhabiting the fastnesses of the mountains on the borders between England and Scotland. This clan, according to the custom of their class, were in the habit of making depredations upon the adjacent villages on either side, pillaging and murdering the inhabitants without mercy. On one occasion, the clan, headed by the chief, who was called the "Raven" on account of his portending death and destruction wherever he made his appearance, burst in upon a hall in Scotland where a newly-married couple of distinction were celebrating their wedding banquet. The chief, after violating the bride in the presence of the bridegroom, murdered her. A desperate conflict took place between the borderers and the bridegroom and his retainers, the result of which was that all the former were slain, the chief only escaping. The sequel is related in the poem.

b.—THE BIRD OF PARADISE.—Page 16.

This piece derives its origin from a legend which the author read describing a monk as wandering from a convent one beautiful spring morning into the country. The monk felt himself impelled by an unaccountable curiosity, to proceed further and further until he became overwhelmed with delight and amazement at the extraordinary beauty that assumed. Suddenly he entered an enchanted forest, nature illuminated with supernatural light, and replete with ambrosial odours. Overcome by emotion, he threw himself on the sward beneath a spreading tree, when suddenly there arose sounds of such inexpressibly delightful melody from a bird which was perched overhead, that the monk, so the legend says, fell into an ecstatic trance which lasted a hundred years. The author believes that Longfellow has written on the same subject, but he thinks it is due to himself to say that he never even heard of that production until years after this was composed.

c.—ADDRESS TO BYRON.—Page 53.

By using the word "pure" in describing the characteristics of Lord Byron, the author is conscious of perhaps laying himself open to some little criticism, considering the equivocal reputation which the noble poet bears for morality. But what he means to imply, and which he thinks will be readily admitted by all impartial persons, is that the main tendency of his compositions was decidedly pure, and that where he devoted himself to the more legitimate object of poetry he abounded in pure and elevated sentiment to a pre-eminent degree.

d.—PRAYER.—Page 70.

This idea is not original.

e.—TO A BEAUTIFUL YOUNG LADY.—Page 78.

The author by this sentiment means to convey the idea that Cupid himself would be so captivated with the young lady's charms as to be deprived of the inclination or the power, or both to inspire a passion for that particular object, either in the breast of the author, or in that of any other mortal.

Printed by J. G. CAMPBELL & Co., Press Lane, Sunderland.

www.ingramcontent.com/pod-product-compliance
Lightning Source LLC
Chambersburg PA
CBHW032357020726
47499CB00008B/2797